Scaredy Ghost

Slowly, Scaredy floated up the stairs. When he had almost reached the top, an owl hooted loudly in the garden. Scaredy nearly fell over the bannisters but, taking a deep breath, on he went...

With a trembling hand he pushed open the door of the children's bedroom and loomed in...

If you're *really* brave, there are all these other Young Hippo Spookies to enjoy!

Ghost Dog
Ghost Horse
Eleanor Allen

Mystery Valentine
Carol Barton

The Screaming Demon Ghostie
Jean Chapman

The Ghost of Able Mabel
Penny Dolan

The Ghost Hunter
Ivan Jones

The Green Hand
Tessa Krailing

Smoke Cat
Linda Newbery

Bumps in the Night
Frank Rodgers

Spooky Movie
Claire Ronan

The Kings' Castle
Ann Ruffell

Scarem's House
Malcolm Yorke

ANGELA MCALLISTER

Scaredy Ghost

Illustrated by Susie Jenkin-Pearce

Scholastic Children's Books,
Commonwealth House, 1-19 New Oxford Street,
London WC1A 1NU, UK
a division of Scholastic Ltd
London ~ New York ~ Toronto ~ Sydney ~ Auckland

Published in the UK by Scholastic Ltd, 1998

Text copyright © Angela McAllister, 1998
Illustrations copyright © Susie Jenkin-Pearce, 1998

ISBN 0 590 19680 4

Printed by Cox & Wyman Ltd, Reading, Berks.

2 4 6 8 10 9 7 5 3 1

Scaredy Ghost

Chapter 1

Scaredy Ghost was eight years old and it was time for him to take the Junior Ghost Exam.

Scaredy had studied hard at school but still didn't feel ready. He had practised making himself invisible but always forgot his nose or a toe. He could walk through walls, but often came out in the wrong place. Poor Scaredy just wasn't confident at all.

His mother and father taught him everything they knew.

"It's very easy to frighten people," said Scaredy's father, taking his head off and putting it under his arm. "And it's lots of fun!"

"You can do anything, Scaredy," his mother promised, "if you only believe that you can."

But Scaredy didn't believe he could frighten people, because he was frightened of everything himself.

"I am terrified of spiders, loud noises make me jump, and I run away from shadows. Worst of all, I'm afraid of the dark! Who would ever be frightened of me?" he sighed glumly.

"Well, tomorrow night you must take the first part of the Ghost Test," said his father. "You will have to haunt a family asleep in their beds, using all the spooky things you have learnt. There is still one more day left to practise, son. Just think scary thoughts." Then, "BOO!" he shouted at the top of his voice. "That spooked you!" He went off with his laughing head still under his arm.

"I know I must keep trying and not give up," Scaredy sighed to himself. So before it got dark that evening he went out to practise.

First he found a small kitten curled up in a wheelbarrow of grass cuttings. Creeping close he made a sudden ugly face … but the kitten wasn't frightened at all. It only purred, licked his nose and turned over to be stroked.

"Oh, I'm useless!" said Scaredy crossly.

Next, he walked through the wall of a house and jumped out at an old lady in her bath. Scaredy wailed like a banshee, but the old lady just cackled with laughter. "Get him, rubber duckie!" she shouted and shot him with her water pistol.

Finally, Scaredy put his head under his arm and poked his tongue out at a baby. But the baby simply smiled and cooed, "Goo-goo, ga-ga gooooo…" and hit him on the head with a rattle!

Poor Scaredy felt a dreadful failure. "Nobody is scared of me. I shall never pass my test tomorrow," he sighed as he trudged home.

Scaredy was so downhearted that he didn't notice the work of a busy spider who'd been exploring his porch, and walked straight into a sticky, dew-drippy web. The angry spider prickled down his neck. Ugh! It was a terrible finish to a terrible day!

When he was safely in his room, Scaredy lit the night-light and checked beneath the bed for bogeymen. Then he buried his head under the pillow, went to sleep and had nightmares all night.

The following evening, Scaredy watched the moon come up and his heart sank.

"Time to go for your test, son," said his father, handing him an envelope. "This is the address of the house you must haunt."

Scaredy opened the envelope. Inside was the name of Colonel Fearless and his family who lived at 1, Dreadnought Street.

"Oh dear," said Scaredy's father.

"That's a bit of bad luck, son. The Colonel is a brave explorer. He has seen gruesome things in the jungle, creepy things in the desert, and horrible things at sea, but he says he has never been frightened once."

Scaredy was already afraid of Colonel Fearless.

"Never mind, do your best, son, good luck," said his father with a ghoulish grin, "and remember ... BOO! That spooked you!"

It certainly did.

Poor Scaredy Ghost set off feeling so nervous that his teeth chattered all the way.

Chapter 2

When Scaredy got to 1, Dreadnought Street, the lights were off. The Colonel and his family were already fast asleep after an adventurous day.

Lucky I brought a candle, thought Scaredy as he slipped through a window into the dark house.

He decided to try the easiest test

first and set off to look for the children's room.

Slowly, Scaredy floated up the stairs. When he had almost reached the top, an owl hooted loudly in the garden. Scaredy nearly fell over the bannisters but, taking a deep breath, on he went…

With a trembling hand, he pushed open the door of the children's bedroom and loomed in…

Three stern little faces frowned on their pillows. Scaredy rattled the windows and creaked the floorboards, but the children didn't stir. Then he pulled out his ball and chain and dragged it clanking around the bed, but the children just sniffed and snored.

Suddenly, Scaredy had a feeling that something behind him was watching. It was something spooky and it was getting closer... Very slowly, he peered over his shoulder and saw ... his own huge shadow up on the wall!

WHAAAAGH!!!

Scaredy gave a terrified scream and flew out of the room, waking up all the children.

Leaping through the door at the end of the hall, Scaredy found himself in Grandpa's room. He paused to catch his breath. Grandpa slept with his eyes open and a spear under the bed. Strange masks grinned horribly on the walls.

Scaredy crossed his fingers and flew around Grandpa's bed, swaying up close with grim ghoulish faces. But Grandpa just twitched his nose and didn't even blink an eye. Then Scaredy pulled off the bedclothes and made them fly around the room like wild kites. But Grandpa always slept with a woolly vest under his pyjamas, so he didn't even shiver.

Scaredy was wondering what else might give Grandpa a fright when he heard a rustle in the corner of the room. Scaredy froze. There was silence again and then muffled scratchy sounds… He crept close with his candle and saw … Grandpa's tarantula collection!

YAAAARGH!!!

Scaredy gave a petrified shout and flew out of the room, waking Grandpa and shattering all the windows in the house!

He escaped next door into the bedroom of Colonel and Mrs Fearless. The Colonel, snoring through his whiskers like a roaring lion, lay beside Mrs Fearless, who was wearing earplugs.

Scaredy wished he was at home, snoring in his own bed. His knees were knocking and his tummy was squirming, but he raised his arms and swooped down with his most blood-curdling wail. Colonel Fearless smiled as though he was having a happy dream and Mrs Fearless rolled over with a sigh.

Suddenly Scaredy gasped. A big, hairy moth flew through the window and flickered around the candle. Scaredy was terrified of moths. He watched in horror as it danced round the flame and then flew across the room and landed on the Colonel's nose.

The Colonel snored, then he snorted, then he sneezed "Aaaaatishooo!" and blew the candle out.

Everything went dark. Scaredy gave a horrified scream:

EEEERGH!!!

He crashed three times round the room and out of the door, waking up the Colonel and Mrs Fearless.

Down the stairs Scaredy flew,
straight into a great cobweb.

OOOOAAAARGH!!!

he wailed, toppling into the cellar,
which was full of mice.

YIIIIPES!!!

he cried, tearing out of a window where hundreds of bats were flying.

GHAAARGH!!!

he bawled and fled down the street, not looking back until he was safe at last under his own bed!

Poor Scaredy had never been so frightened in all his life.

Chapter 3

In the morning Scaredy's father found him still under the bed, fast asleep.

"Wake up, son," he laughed, "you've got visitors!"

With a shudder, Scaredy remembered the night before. How was he going to explain to his father how badly he had done?

Scaredy crept out from under the bed, but before he could finish a yawn, Colonel Fearless appeared and shook him by the hand.

"Congratulations," said the Colonel. "We've never been so frightened in our lives. The children fell out of their beds, Grandpa's still covered in goosebumps, our hair turned white, the cat had kittens and the neighbours say they will never set foot in our house again! We were terrified, horrified, absolutely petrified! Jolly well done. Full marks!"

Scaredy didn't know what to say.

The Colonel handed him the Junior Ghost Certificate and a large box of Spooky Tricks. "Just promise never to visit our house again, young man," he laughed. "And now Mrs Fearless and I are off to buy some hair-dye and a large cat basket."

"Well done, Scaredy," said his father when the Colonel had gone. "I don't know what you did last night, but it seems that you frightened the whole neighbourhood. Your mother and I are really proud of you."

Scaredy grinned. "I'll whisper you my secret, Dad," he said mysteriously. His father bent close.

"You see … BOO! That spooked you!" shouted Scaredy Ghost.

And to his father's delight, it did!

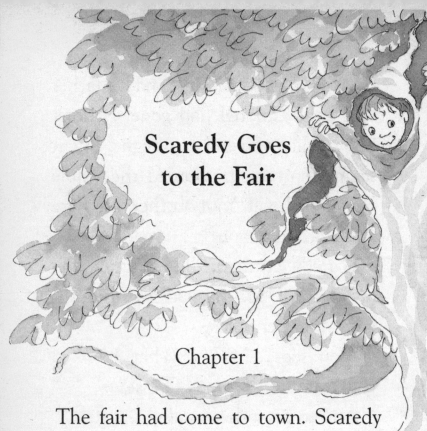

Scaredy Goes to the Fair

Chapter 1

The fair had come to town. Scaredy spent all afternoon hidden up a tree in the park, watching the men set up their stalls and build the big wheel and the helter-skelter. He couldn't wait to bump on the dodgems and eat sticky candyfloss when the fair opened that night.

But after tea, when it was time for the fair to begin, Scaredy's father wouldn't let him go.

"A little ghost cannot go to the fair, son," he said. "It would cause Terrible Trouble."

"But that's unfair!" cried Scaredy.

"Not UNfair," grinned his father, "NO fair! I'm sorry. Why don't we play dominoes instead?"

Scaredy didn't want to play dominoes. He wanted to sulk and feel very cross. His mother said there was only one place for sulking and sent him to bed.

Scaredy lay on his bed, frowning hard. Outside, he could hear the fairground music and children laughing as they whizzed on the rides.

"Suppose I just went for a walk…" said Scaredy to himself. "Nobody said I couldn't go for a walk. Nobody causes Terrible Trouble just going for a walk…"

So, deciding not to tell his father, Scaredy walked straight through his bedroom wall and out into the street!

The street was busy with excited people eating toffee-apples and showing prizes they had won. Scaredy kept out of sight. Since he'd passed the Junior Ghost Test he was no longer frightened of the dark, so he crept through the shadows until he found himself at the park.

Scaredy climbed the tree again and watched the bright lights and painted stalls. Nearby, a rocket ride zoomed high in the sky, plunged down as though it was going to crash, and then spun round safely just at the last minute. Everybody screamed but they queued up to go again.

Scaredy crept closer and closer along a branch to see … until with a great crack the branch split and he fell over the fence into a bush in the fairground.

"Well, they said I couldn't go to the fair, but they didn't mention accidentally *falling* into it…" he said to himself as he crawled out of the bush. "Now I'm here I'll just have a look at that rocket ride…"

Chapter 2

And so Scaredy went to the fair.

At first no one noticed him join the crowd by the rocket ride. But when he walked right through the barrier and sat in the front seat someone shouted, "It's a ghost!" and a tall, skinny man with freckles fainted on the spot.

Before the ticket man could

investigate, the rocket launched upwards and Scaredy felt his tummy flip like a pancake in a pan.

"YIIIPPPES!" he screamed on the way up and, "YUUUUEEERRPPPP!" he screamed on the way down.

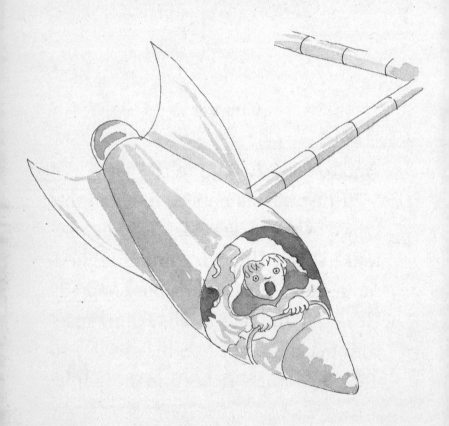

Then, "CRRIIKEY!" he cried as the rocket returned to the launch pad, where Scaredy saw the ticket collector looking very angry indeed. He decided to get off early, jumped out of his seat and landed behind the Hall of Mirrors.

Scaredy opened a side door into the Hall of Mirrors and crept in. People giggled at themselves looking fat in one mirror and thin in another.

They laughed at each other's big noses and jug ears. But they didn't expect their hair to stand on end until a ghost appeared, sticking his tongue out in the mirror behind them! Before you could say, "Who is the fairest of them all?" the Hall of Mirrors was empty!

Scaredy had great fun all alone, practising his most frightful faces, which looked even more gruesome than usual. Then he decided to find himself some candyfloss.

However, when Scaredy saw the candyfloss stall he realized that he had no money. Children queued with their coins to buy the sticks of pink and white sugar fluff. Scaredy wanted some very badly.

"If *I* had some candyfloss I would be very happy to share it…" Scaredy explained to himself, as an idea came into his head. "I'm sure everybody feels like that." And creeping round the side of the stall, he hid until a child walked by. Then, as the candyfloss passed right before his eyes he stretched out a long, ghostly tongue and took a lick!

However, Scaredy was so busy sucking the sticky sugar from his lips that he didn't notice two strong men searching all over the fairground…

"Have you seen the ghost?" they asked people waiting to ride the dodgems. "No!" the people cried excitedly, and they left the queue to join the hunt. Soon a great crowd was looking for Scaredy.

Just as a shiny toffee-apple came within reach of Scaredy's long tongue, he heard a gruff voice shout, "Hey, you! Come here at once!"

Oh dear, thought Scaredy. I think this is the beginning of the Terrible Trouble!

Quick as a flash, he slipped through some railings and jumped into a dodgem. With sparks flying, Scaredy raced round and round, bumping all the cars. When the other drivers saw they were being chased by a ghost, they screamed and put their hands over their eyes! Scaredy had never had such fun, but the dodgem boys were jumping from car to car to find who was causing all the trouble...

"Time to go!" cried Scaredy, and he escaped to the helter-skelter.

Picking up a hairy mat, Scaredy climbed the steps up the helter-skelter. By the time he looked out from the top of the slide, a great crowd had gathered to catch him below. "You wait here at the bottom, Fred," said one of the fairground men. "I'm going up..."

"Now I'm in for it," Scaredy said to himself. He knew there was no turning back. So, with a banshee wail, he launched himself down the slide, twisting high above the fairground, and just before the bottom he flew into the air and loomed low over the gasping crowd.

Scaredy was having the time of his

life. He flew circles with the Ferris wheel, he swooped and dived with the big dipper, and he scared all the people on the merry-go-round.

Then, spotting more tempting candyfloss, he glided down among the stalls and was promptly caught in a fishing net! "Got you!" exclaimed a rather plump skeleton.

Fred and his mate came running up. "Well done, Bones," they said, and untangled Scaredy from the net.

Chapter 3

Scaredy Ghost looked around and realized what he had done: Children were crying over their stolen candyfloss, some people had fainted, and the rides were empty because a great crowd was wandering around the fairground looking for a ghost. Scaredy felt very bad. He'd only wanted to have some fun, but now he saw that his father had been right – a ghost couldn't go to the fair without causing Terrible Trouble. "I'm very sorry, Mr Bones," he said to the man in the skeleton suit. "My dad told me that I couldn't come to the fair so I sneaked out. He's going to be very cross when I get home."

Fred, Bones and their mate looked at each other and laughed.

"We are very glad that you came to the fair," they said. "We've never met a

real ghost before." Bones made a little bow. "We run the Ghost Train, you see," he explained. "We don't want to get you into trouble. We want you to help us."

Scaredy didn't understand.

"It's very simple," said Fred. "If we could promise there would be a *real* ghost on our train we'd be a sell-out every day. People love to be frightened at the fair, and with you to scare them we'd have queues at the gate."

Scaredy was very relieved that he wasn't going to get into Terrible Trouble – at least until he got home.

"If you scare people on our train we'll get you free rides on everything else at the fair," said Bones.

"Will there be candyfloss, too?" asked Scaredy.

"Oh, clouds of candyfloss," laughed Fred. And so it was agreed.

"You can start tomorrow morning," said Fred. "Meet us by the Ghost Train at ten o'clock and we'll show you what to do."

When Scaredy got home he did get into Terrible Trouble. His mother and father had been worried when they'd discovered he was gone. Scaredy told them he was sorry.

"I promise never to wander out through my bedroom wall again," he said.

"Well, as you are so keen on walls, son, you can help me paint the bedrooms," said his dad. "And there'll be no pocket money until they are all finished." Scaredy agreed. Then he explained what Fred and Bones had asked him to do.

"I've learnt that I can't visit crowded places without scaring people," he said. "But the Ghost Train is one place where people actually go to be frightened."

Scaredy's dad didn't want to stop him from having fun.

"All right, you can go," he said. "If the fair is as exciting as you say, your mum and I might come along ourselves, one evening…"

And so Scaredy started the very next day.

Fred and Bones made a huge poster

THE ONLY
GHOST TRAIN
WITH A REAL GHOST
ARE YOU BRAVE ENOUGH TO RIDE?

– and crowds of excited people were soon daring each other to have a go.

At first, as the train rolled into the spooky tunnel, nobody would notice Scaredy sitting in the front carriage – until he took off his head and turned it backwards to grin at the passengers! Then he would fly above them, letting rip a terrifying wail, and the journey would begin.

All day, Scaredy leapt through walls and loomed out of the darkness, having a wild and wonderful time. The people screeched and screamed and then queued up to be scared all over again.

On the last day, Scaredy proudly took his mum and dad on the Ghost Train. When the word went round

that there were *three* real ghosts, *everyone* wanted to ride on the train!

"Well, you have certainly made lots of friends, Scaredy," said his father proudly.

"He's done a grand job. The fair has never been so busy," said Fred. "You must come again, Scaredy, next time we're in town."

Scaredy's mum agreed. "It seems to me that the fair is a very fine place for a Scaredy Ghost, after all!"

Scaredy's Holiday

Chapter 1

Scaredy had been invited to spend the holidays with Uncle McGhoul, who lived in a castle in Scotland. Scaredy had never been to the castle before. "Will I be able to wear a suit of armour and play the bagpipes?" he asked his father excitedly. "And will there be dungeons and secret passages?"

"I'm afraid your uncle is terribly old," said Scaredy's father. "He still does a bit of haunting, but he likes to live a quiet life. So pack lots of books and jigsaws."

However, when Scaredy arrived at Gloom Castle, things were far from quiet. As he walked up the drive, he heard children shouting and a lawnmower splutter. Close to the castle, the sound of bagpipes and screams came from the windows.

"Surely old Uncle McGhoul can't be having a children's party and mowing the lawn and playing the bagpipes and screaming like a banshee *and* having a quiet life all at once?" Scaredy mused.

Then over the gate he saw a flashing sign…

Scaredy decided to investigate, so he made himself invisible and slipped inside.

Sure enough, the great hall of the castle had been turned into a hotel reception. A map on the wall showed where the haunting took place.

"Every bedroom has a ghost," it boasted. "Meet the White Lady and the Phantom of the Portrait. Hear the Screaming Skull at three-thirty every afternoon, and have your photo taken with the Headless Horseman. Golf course, bouncy castle and disco in the dungeon."

Scaredy thought he must have come to the wrong place, but just as he turned to go, a rough boy in football boots ran though the door and into the reception office. Scaredy followed.

"Dad," the boy blubbered to a fat man sitting at the desk, "a ghost tripped me over and took my ball!"

The man was counting piles of money. He looked cross at being disturbed.

"Don't come and tell *me* when you see a ghost," he snapped. "I've told you a hundred times before – tell the guests. The more ghosts they see, or *think* they see, the more they will come back and bring their friends and spend their lovely money." He grinned. "Run into the lounge and tell everyone that you saw a ghost on the stairs holding a dagger dripping with blood. Here…" he pulled a bottle of tomato ketchup from his drawer, "smear yourself with this first."

"But that's a lie, Dad," said the boy.

"No, that's *business*, Dennis," said his dad, grinning wider. "No ghost, no new football, eh?"

Scaredy watched as the poor boy smeared tomato sauce over his arms and trudged off reluctantly to the lounge.

At that moment, a voice whispered in Scaredy's ear. "Pssst! Over here!" And there hiding behind a potted palm was Old Uncle McGhoul himself. "Come on, Scaredy, follow me…"

Uncle McGhoul took Scaredy up a steep spiral staircase that went to the top of the tower. The last step stopped at a stone wall, but Uncle McGhoul passed straight through the wall, and Scaredy followed him into a secret room that no one else had discovered.

"I'm sorry not to give you a proper welcome, laddie," he said when he had caught his breath. "Things have got very difficult around here. It's not my old home any more, as you see."

"What has happened?" asked Scaredy, helping his uncle into an armchair.

Uncle McGhoul sighed. "Well, one day a nosy tourist called Ned Nerd was taking a walk and discovered the castle. He came back after dark to poke around and caught me haunting the battlements. Straight away he bought the place, which had been a peaceful empty ruin for two hundred years. Then he fixed it up and turned it into this dreadful hotel which is always full of people who want to see a ghost. There hasn't been a moment's peace since."

"But where did all the other ghosts come from – the White Lady, and the Headless Horseman?" asked Scaredy. "Are they my relations, too?"

"Oh no, no, nothing could be further from the truth," said Uncle McGhoul with a dark frown. "You see, they're not real ghosts at all! They are Ned Nerd's tricks – along with the sound of banshees wailing and blood appearing

on the stairs and skeletons falling out of cupboards. When he saw that he could make money here he didn't want to depend on one old ghost.

"He will do anything to deceive people for his profits. Everything's fake except your old uncle. I've never been so miserable in my life. The castle is full of noisy, snooping people, the whole place smells of chips and at night a horrible howling shakes the dungeons. Even my bats have had enough and left home. It's unbearable."

Scaredy felt very sorry for poor Uncle McGhoul. "Can't you come and live with us instead?" he asked. Uncle McGhoul smiled.

"You're a thoughtful, kind boy, Scaredy. But you see it's my fate to haunt this castle for ever. I'm four hundred and ninety-three next Wednesday and all I want is a quiet life and my old home to myself, but there is nothing I can do to get rid of Ned Nerd."

Suddenly, a hair-raising scream came from the hall. Uncle McGhoul groaned. "That means dinner is served," he sighed. "Why can't they just ring a little tinkling bell? Well, at least while everyone is in the restaurant I can give you a tour of the castle. Come on, laddie!"

Uncle McGhoul showed Scaredy all the rooms and secret passages in the castle.

"Your great-aunt Mathilda kept crocodiles here in the moat," he said. "I always hope one might still be lying in the mud at the bottom and will leap out one day and gobble up a few guests…"

Then he showed Scaredy a four-poster bed.

"This was made specially for your cousin Gordon, two hundred years ago."

Scaredy climbed up to see if it was a good bouncer.

"Be careful, laddie!" warned Uncle McGhoul. "There's a trap-door in the mattress for visitors who snore too loudly! They were sent down a shute into the dungeon where no one could hear them. So far, I've sent forty-eight hotel guests down the shute and no one has discovered the secret!"

In the armour room, Scaredy tried on some chain-mail and Uncle McGhoul showed him how to use a sword. Although Uncle McGhoul was old, he was still a nimble swordsman and they were soon enjoying a heroic fight. They didn't notice dinner was over until Ned Nerd's son Dennis came in.

When Uncle McGhoul saw the enemy he raised his sword and swooped around the boy. "Beware the blade of McGhoul of Gloom!" he wailed, and the poor boy ran out, white as a sheet.

For the first time that day, Scaredy saw old Uncle McGhoul laugh. "It's great fun having you here, Scaredy," he said. "It makes me feel young again. Maybe together we can beat Ned Nerd and his horrible guests."

And Scaredy promised he would think of a way…

After the tour, Scaredy and his uncle returned to the secret tower and had to content themselves by quietly doing a jigsaw while mysterious wailings echoed through the castle walls. When it was time for bed, Scaredy couldn't sleep. He lay awake trying to think of a way to help his unhappy uncle…

Chapter 2

In the morning, Scaredy set off to explore the dungeons. A sign said "To the Disco" so he went in the opposite direction. The damp, slimy passages snaked far underground. Scaredy thought hard about Uncle McGhoul's problem and didn't notice how far he'd walked, until he stepped out of a cave into a creepy wood. Climbing through the undergrowth, he came to a dark lake. The water was deep and murky and a mist floated mysteriously above it.

Maybe this is Loch Ness, he thought nervously. It looks just the sort of place for a serpent to hide…

Something rustled in the bushes nearby… Suddenly, Scaredy felt alone and very small. He didn't want to meet the Loch Ness monster. He wanted to be safe at the Haunted Hotel, so he flew back to the castle like the wind!

Uncle McGhoul laughed when he heard where Scaredy had been. "No, that isn't Loch Ness. It's Loch Gloom. We don't have any monsters round here! You shouldn't believe in nonsense like that, laddie."

Scaredy felt silly but he couldn't get Loch Gloom out of his mind all afternoon.

The next day, while Ned Nerd was in the village putting his bags of money in the bank, a poster appeared in the hotel reception.

At the bottom was a drawing of a fierce serpent in green crayon.

"This is weird…" said Uncle McGhoul. "I've lived here for four hundred years and there's never been anything in the loch but mud, minnows and old boots."

"Well, shall we go and see?" said Scaredy excitedly, and they took the short cut through the dungeon passage.

Several of the hotel guests had come to the loch with picnics and binoculars, hoping to see the monster. But while nothing was happening they were playing Frisbee and skimming stones on the water.

"Nothing will appear while they're making all that hullabaloo," groaned Uncle McGhoul. "Let's go home, Scaredy." But Scaredy had wandered off somewhere.

Then, before Uncle McGhoul's eyes, the water of the loch began to ripple and a long, lizard-like creature raised its head and gave a roar.

The children screamed and people dropped their sausage rolls in astonishment.

"Wow! A real sea serpent!"

screamed a lady in a pink headscarf, who then fell off a rock into the water. Two men helped her hurriedly out.

"One more moment in that loch and I might have been eaten alive," she spluttered as she caught her breath. "This is *much* more thrilling than a dusty old ghost. Look, look!"

All the hotel guests were glued to their cameras excitedly. The monster glided in a circle through the water as if it knew it was being photographed.

Then it dipped and dived, and with a splash it was gone as suddenly as it had appeared.

"I'm going to camp out here tonight," said the wet lady to the crowd. "I don't want to miss anything. Get Mr Nerd to send my dinner on a tray."

Now there was a monster about, Uncle McGhoul was worried that Scaredy might be lost and in danger. "Where are you, laddie?" he cried through the woods. "You've missed the serpent … it might not appear again for five hundred years!"

But little did he know the monster would appear again much sooner than that.

"Psst!" said a voice a moment later from the bushes. "Over here…"

When Uncle McGhoul turned round he saw Scaredy dripping wet, draped in the long green curtains from the tower room, and wearing a serpent mask that looked as if it was made from an old waste-paper basket!

"Loch Gloom monster at your service." He grinned and gave a quiet roar.

"You see, I have a plan," explained Scaredy when Uncle McGhoul had recovered from his surprise. "I have a feeling Castle Gloom will soon return to its old quiet life. And this afternoon we'll take a trip to the pet shop to replace your bats that flew away. If my plan works you shall be saying 'good riddance' to Ned Nerd very soon."

But Scaredy would say no more than that…

Chapter 3

By the next morning, every guest at the hotel, every porter and chambermaid had heard about the monster of Loch Gloom. Nobody was in the restaurant for breakfast; they'd all gone to catch a glimpse of "Gloomie" as they'd decided to call it. And as there were no guests, the staff decided to take the day off and have a look for themselves.

By the time Ned Nerd came down to his office, the castle was completely deserted. All he found was a hurried note from Dennis:

dere DAd gON tO thE LOk To ?ee tHe MOnSTa

and so he set off to see the attraction for himself…

Down on the loch, Gloomie made another appearance, this time to a great gasping crowd. He roared and thrashed his tail and a hundred cameras flashed. But while the excited tourists watched the monster, Ned Nerd was watching them…

The third morning, Uncle McGhoul was woken up by the sound of hammering at the gate. When he looked out of the window, he saw Ned Nerd putting up a sign saying

Scaredy rushed in, full of excitement. "My plan has worked," he cheered. "Ned Nerd is putting the castle up for sale and building a new hotel down by the Loch immediately. It's going to be called 'Serpent's Watch!'"

Uncle McGhoul did a jig around the tower. "That's terrific news, laddie." But then he looked worried. "What will they do when you go home and there's no Gloomie any more?"

"You will just have to disguise yourself as I did and float about the lake once in a while to keep them all keen," laughed Scaredy. "Anyway, Ned Nerd will soon be thinking up all sorts of tricks the way he did at the castle to keep his guests coming. I saw plans on his desk to build mechanical submarine serpents, just like the fake ghosts, so after a while you won't even have to make an appearance at all!"

And sure enough, before long Loch Gloom was busy with monsters and serpents splashing and roaring day and night. People came from far and wide to take pictures and make a lot of noise. But on the far side of the woods Uncle McGhoul didn't hear a thing.

To his delight Castle Gloom remained unsold and grew dim and dusty once more. Happy bats flitted about the battlements and Scaredy returned to spend his holidays there every summer, with his favourite uncle – Uncle McGhoul.

The End